Lisette The Vet

Ruth MacPete, DVM

Illustrations by Anzhelika Enshina

Lisette the Vet

First Printing, 2018
Library of Congress Control Number: 2018943827
ISBN 978-0-9996735-1-5

Forest Lane Books
PO Box 371006
San Diego, CA 92137

Art done by hand and completed using Photoshop
Typeset in Century Schoolbook and Chiller

Production supervision by Henry Ferreyra
Typography by Clark Kenyon
Illustrations by Anzhelika Enshina

Dedicated to the Lisettes of the world who dream of becoming a vet someday, and to my amazing family and friends who have always encouraged me to follow my dreams.

Lisette the Vet, that's what her friends called her
because she wanted to be a vet when she grew up.

She had three cats, two dogs, a parrot, and a
frog. Her friends joked that she lived in a zoo.

Lisette loved to read.
She had read every
book about animals in
the library.

But most importantly,
Lisette LOVED animals:

big or little,

furry or feathery,

even slimy or scaly.

All animals except...

Lisette did NOT like spiders. They were hairy, creepy and just plain scary.

Lisette's class was getting
a pet tomorrow. She could
hardly wait. She hoped
it would be a bunny; or a
hamster; or a gecko.

That morning Lisette woke up extra early. She skipped the playground and ran straight to class.

There was already a crowd.
She peered over them but
couldn't see, so she squeezed
in for a closer look.

Lisette nearly fell over! Eight beady eyes stared back at
her from the biggest, hairiest spider she had ever seen.

"Meet Fluffy," said Mr. Webster.
"He's our Mexican Red Knee
Tarantula."
"Really?" Lisette asked. "Of all the
possible pets, we get a big ugly
spider?"

"He's awesome!" Ethan
shouted.
"Disgusting," Lisette
mumbled.

All day all everyone talked about was Fluffy.

"Look," Julia said, "Fluffy's eating a cricket."

"Wow," Henry pointed out, "he's hiding under the log."

"Whoa," John cried, "Fluffy's sleeping!"

Everyone was so
excited...except Lisette.
She was so over Fluffy.

The Complete Guide
to Animals

Then IT happened.

Ethan screamed,
"Emory dropped Fluffy!"
"Oh no!" Devon cried.
"Is he dead?" asked Siena.
"What do we do?" Emory asked.
Lisette couldn't help but look.

She put down her book and peeked over Devon's shoulder.

Fluffy was upside down and he wasn't moving.

Then a leg twitched.

"He's still alive," Siena shouted.

"Somebody please do something!" Ethan pleaded.

Everyone looked around, but no one moved.

Lisette knew Fluffy needed help.
She stepped forward for a closer look. Fluffy really was hairy,
and a bit creepy, but he wasn't as scary as she thought.

Yellow goo oozed from one of his legs. Lisette looked closely at Fluffy.

I know what's wrong, she thought.

I remember reading that tarantulas have yellow blood and super glue can be used to stop bleeding.

"I need super glue," Lisette yelled.

"Super glue? Why?" Ethan asked.

"Just trust me," she said.

Mr. Webster
handed Lisette
the glue.
She took a deep
breath, steadied
her hand, and
slowly squeezed
a drop of glue on
Fluffy's injured
leg.

Lisette and her classmates
watched silently. No one
moved. Seconds passed.

Finally, the bleeding stopped and Fluffy started to move. "He's going to be okay," Lisette shouted.

"You saved Fluffy," Devon cried.
"Hooray for Lisette the Vet!" everyone cheered.

As her class celebrated, Lisette let Fluffy climb up her hand.

"You know, spiders aren't as bad as I thought," Lisette told Ethan. "And being super smart isn't so bad either," Ethan whispered with a smile. But Lisette already knew that!

LISETTE THE VET'S TARANTULA FUN FACTS

- There are more than 800 different species of tarantulas.
- They are found on every continent except Antarctica.
- Tarantulas live in burrows not webs. Although they do not spin webs, they line their burrows with silk.
- Tarantulas are carnivores. They eat insects, beetles and grasshoppers. Some of the larger species can even eat frogs, lizards and small birds.
- To a person, tarantula venom is weaker than a bee sting.
- Tarantulas are most active at night (nocturnal).

- Tarantulas use their legs to catch their prey and their fangs to inject venom to paralyze them. They inject digestive enzymes to turn their prey into a liquid meal.
- Tarantulas can live up to 30 years.
- When threatened, tarantulas can shoot barbed hairs from their abdomen at the face and eyes of their attackers.
- Tarantulas have retractable claws like cats.
- And of course, tarantulas have yellow blood and super glue can be used to stop bleeding!

About the Author

Dr. Ruth MacPete is a practicing
veterinarian and the author of *Lisette the
Vet*. Like Lisette, she loved animals and
wanted to be a vet for as long as she could
remember. She grew up with dogs, cats,
hamsters, guinea pigs, rabbits, fish, birds,
and even a chinchilla. Growing up, she cared
for the neighborhood's injured, orphaned, and
abandoned animals. She is grateful for being
able to do what she loves and she wants
to encourage all children to follow their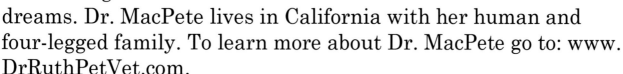
dreams. Dr. MacPete lives in California with her human and
four-legged family. To learn more about Dr. MacPete go to: www.
DrRuthPetVet.com.

Made in the USA
Monee, IL
04 December 2020